Territory
of
Wind

For Gail

Territories of
Poetry to you

5/99

Territory of Wind

poems by
patrice vecchione

MANY NAMES PRESS
SANTA CRUZ, CALIFORNIA

Poems in this collection have appeared, some in earlier versions, in the following anthologies and periodicals: *Bless Me Father: Stories of Catholic Childhood*: "Anger's Gift"; *Catholic Girls: Stories, Poems, and Memoirs*: "First Communion"; *Ikon*: "Astoria, New York, 1988"; *In Celebration of the Muse: Writings By Santa Cruz Women*: "Our Private Air," "A Month Later"; *In Celebration of the Muse: the Fifteenth Anniversary Anthology*: "Her Face in the Trees"; *The Lavender Reader*: "When Grief Moves In"; *The No-Child Poems* (a chapbook): "No-Child Has A Mother," "No-Child Has A Father"; *Lovers*: "What Grandmother Wants"; *Porter Gulch Review*: "Anger's Gift" (winner of the Mary Lonnberg Smith Award), "At the Gateway to Desolation Wilderness," "Hot Springs At Colusa," "Kitchen Table Waltz," "Salt," "Toward the Only Sky"; *Puerto Del Sol*: "Lost and Found"; *Red Dirt*: "Nine Months"; *Quarry West*: "Sotto, Sotto"; *The Santa Cruz County Sentinel*: "August's Full Moon," "Near Spring"; *Storming Heaven's Gate: Spiritual Writings by Women*: "Toward the Only Sky"; *The 1994 Women Writers Calendar*: "Hot Springs At Colusa."

Acknowledgments

For sustenance, poetic and otherwise, I wish to thank Ali Bermond, Joshua Gardner, Nicholas Gardner, Rae Grad, Janet Greenberg, Pamela Jones, Maude Meehan, Nancy Norris, Mary Quinton, Gael Roziere, Barbara Stark, Jolene Stark, Roy Stark, Kyle VanWest, Nicholas Vecchione, Diana Wertz, Canon Western, and Alison Winterle; for their inspiration, past and present, Susan Griffin, Ani Mander, and Adrienne Rich; for introducing me to the physio-spiritual virtues of the bicycle, Michael Mason. In memory of Lynn Luria-Sukenick, her grace and friendship. Remembering my uncle Lou Piliero. I am grateful to Kate Hitt for the elegance of her work. To Nanda Currant for her artwork which graces this book's cover and for her friendship. To Carol Stoneburner for her precision. To Carol Staudacher and Steve Wiesinger for their many at-the-last-minute-hours, their care and attention to detail. For being my longtime partner in poetry and the making of books, I wish to acknowledge Amber Coverdale Sumrall.

—P.V.

For Michael Stark,
Wendy Traber,
and
Gina Van Horn

And in memory of my mother,
Peggy Vecchione

Contents

I

II

III

I

They are not pictures. I have made a place.
—Mark Rothko

Invisible

Though I placed your clothes in the neighborhood
cemetery on the soft grass between the graves
of relatives, you have not come back.
Long nights at the window, I've spent waiting
for you to return, wearing the white shirt,
black pants and shoes. But they, too, are gone
from beside the ivory stones, into the burdened
mouths of the night songbirds.

Geography Lesson

Isn't it odd, the effect geography has on the mind?

—*Virginia Woolf*

When they said the Red Sea, I always saw a picture
in my head of Jones Beach, dozens of children
playing out there, their bodies shining
in all that red. And when they said the Black Sea,
I saw the Triboro Bridge, only underneath,
where the metal girders come down and settle
into the sand, how dark it must be there, how cold.

If only I can get him out of my car
everything will be alright. I can go home,
wipe this heaviness off my face.
They say in *that* country women carry
their belongings on the top of their heads.
The pictures in our lesson book showed this:
pomegranate, yellow melons, their weight in gold.

When the truck ran into my car
my teeth began to ache and I saw the Red Sea again.
I told the officer it was at the corner of here
and there. No, I had no passengers, I wasn't
even moving. But the Red Sea is moving, I know this.
And the Black Sea is too. Even the Triboro Bridge
sways over its water as I drive quickly across.

He, the one whose name begins with the alphabet's
every letter, doesn't ride in my car anymore.
He never did after we got to the light
and, like a monkey, I screamed, "Get out."

My body is not a vessel, not a car, not this corner
or that corner. It is the Red Sea moving inside
the Black Sea. It is not the basket.
It is what is carried inside the basket.
And she carries it on the top of her head.

At Wilbur Springs

Even if I wrote for a week, sequestered away
in the oil lit room, I don't think I could loosen
the sadness that is buckled down inside
every breath. At the window, the curtains
gather their lace, fringed like a pony's mane.

Night comes along slowly from someplace
out of this valley. Beside the creek, a man
reads a newspaper. Bending forward,
a woman dries her hair in the fading light.
Soon, I will be able to see nothing. So I dry off,
come inside, stand at the stove preparing dinner
in an orderly manner; only one plate is dirtied
at a time. Having not spoken all day, I am startled
when someone asks my name, blurt out
the familiar syllables, turn away.

Just before night everything turns grey.
Grey sky. Grey in the limbs of trees.
Grey look on the man's face. Grey eyes.
I said to the man at home, who is not
a quiet stranger, a young girl lives here
who sees through the veiled things.
Pulling the curtains back, I've found you.
Go hide and seek.

What have I found this time bucking under
my ribs? How do you write the world
into one poem? Sadness, that indelible ink,
is tattooed across my left breast.
Is it what draws the lover near
or what turns him away?

On stage the other night I stood a breath away
from the microphone, calling out my fat words
and the thin, into the darkness of the beer hall.
The audience sat listening; they were listening
to me. When I took off my jacket,
the one that had belonged to my father
and was tailored to fit me, I pulled my shoulders back,
began juggling words.

I've got a horse up my sleeve, awake
in its fenced corral. It's not a little thing
I've come here for, not a lost medal.
It's what's beneath the saddle,
the neighing, clambering, biting thing.

Or Is It Autumn Still?

This winter I am losing my hair, or is it autumn still?
Strands and strands of fine brown hair fall through
my fingers. And yet, there is the head of hair
I shake dry or braid with quick fingers.

This is not my mother's hair,
because she had none, nor my father's
which curls black and white away from his face.
My sister's hangs loose and long and blond.

My leg was warm when the tall man reached over
and ran his big hand up and down my thigh.
And then I became warmer, not only my leg,
but all over. For a Wednesday night
the movie theatre was full, and a woman
on the screen was singing.

For a long time I had my eyes closed.
It was for many years I lived that way.
All through school they stayed closed,
except at night alone with cartoon characters
and the Virgin who came to my bed.

Sometimes he touches my hair with his hands,
and I like this. We have only a few sometimes
to look back on. But still I can say, sometimes
his hands are on my hair, this long hair
I am afraid of losing.

After the film, we sat in the car with the heater
warming December. Mostly I had my hands in my lap
or clasped to the steering wheel. And he had his own too.
It was dark all around the car, and I looked out
at the parking lot, the train tracks and the doors
of the buildings that were shut, every one of them.

"What are you looking for?" he asked.
I said, "I am not looking for anything."
That was a thin lie. He could see my eyes
at the window and beyond the window. Could he see
which door I was looking at? Did he see the trees?

I am looking for a great love. One that would catch
the train as it goes by. One that would have a man's
two hands in my hair and his whole lips on my mouth.
One that would break the door down,
making me breathe fast. And fast.

I didn't say this. I closed my eyes,
and still I could see the door. My hands
were in my hair when, facing me, he said "Good
night," and got out of the car, letting some
of the night air inside.

Anywhere

Every time I leave the house
I am afraid I will come back
and home won't be here.

Oh, there will be the same door,
the same ring of trees entering their pink bloom,
with the right number above my door frame.

But when I fit the key in
a strange man comes to the door, bare feet,
only shorts on, and a woman
wearing my chenille bathrobe,
my orange cat rubbing against her legs, purring.

"Where'd you get this key?" he asks.
"What are you saying, this is your home?
We've lived here, five years, my wife and I."

Suddenly I am sorry, terribly sorry.
Sure this was the same door, one time.
On my street the wind blows the same whistle.
A man sharing my bed with a woman
he calls his wife. This does not fit.
Walk away.

Now I turn the key into any door,
trying to remember
if I have lived anywhere.

Lost and Found

Late afternoon, nearly dusk
and we've lost our way in the woods
we know the night will freeze,
lost our way in the *I don't remember.*

If only we'd brought the dogs
who know each trail and how it leads home.
I think of following telephone lines
that cross the meadows, certain of a way
to a road that cars might find.

You know how the story goes:
the children huddle together to fight the cold,
then someone saves them. I will share my jacket
with you and pray all night to keep us warm.

Now here's the rotting field of corn
we passed fresh in summertime, that day
we saw the family of boar.

My feet make their way beside yours
in this tremor of fear, searching
for the house that stands beside the carp lake,
where wood is stacked in the hearth ready for fire.
I can almost hear the dogs panting at the door,
hungry and expectant.

Foxglove

for Wendy and Kyle

There are notes in the binder from before sleep
but I turn away from them, onto another path
that winds backwards through the gold-getting
hills rising up from the valley,
becoming drier each day.

Fresh from a bath, my friend and I
walked this dusty way, came upon flowers
whose name I couldn't remember, growing tall
against a grey wooden fence. When I asked
she lifted up her arm, and with her other hand
seemed to delicately put something on,
her raised arm poised like an animal, quiet and aware
or like a woman dressing. And I knew.

This morning in what shade we could find
tucked in my tiny yards, Kyle and I planted foxglove.
In front of the fence where passion vine
and jasmine grow, she searched the slabs of land
already invested with an assortment of flowers,
saying, "Here's some shade," as I followed
with trowel and watering can, bending down
each time, to dig with her, to place and tamp
the tongue-leafed plants into the earth.

Nearly a year, I told her, we will have to wait
before the flowers appear. Being seven now
she knows something about years, that they are
farther than tomorrow, the distance between
one birthday and the next.

After working, we sat awhile on the bench
facing the day lilies, yellow pansies bordering,
and looked out at our work, until she said,
"I have a poem to write down," and we came inside.
Pen and paper in hand, she bent her head.
Beside her, I remembered what I so often forget,
how a poem is written, waiting for what can't be
waited for, talking in signs, my friend's hands
after a bath, signaling foxglove.

Here in my living room, crowned
with the garden's flowers,
Kyle wrote her words, glistening and firm
as the small, white wedge of stone
that she saved from the dark.

Now

Forty or fifty years from now, the time-saint
will be waiting with the life-sheet,
having recorded each nuance of every second
of my life. At the edge of the sky
he will stand in his black and whites,
saying, "On the 21st of October, in the year 1990,
what were you doing at 8:47 A.M.?
What do you have to say for that minute
of your life and its value?"
I will have to search what memory remains
to recall the very moment when I had heart
and eyes and skin.

Will I remember this Sunday morning,
the basketball's persistent bounce
at the neighborhood park just down the street
and the men's huff, huff breathing as they run
across the court, the sound traveling along
the wide street, their yelling
when the ball goes in?

Or will it not be even this:
The air was cool that autumn morning.
I was alone in the room, the cats were hungry
for breakfast, the telephone rang persistently
and went unanswered.

Will I remember the flu which left me
stranded, crawling like a cat to the one square
of light coming in through the window?
And what of the cats' names?

In the future, what will remain
of this precise now, this October morning,
when again the ballplayers yell and clap?

From my upstairs window,
I know something good is happening
for the men in the park, the net swings back
and forth, sweat shines on their strong bodies,
breath leaves their lungs, whitening the air
in front of their most glorious, most alive faces.
This very second, now.

Buckled briefcase. Pocket. Smocked gingham, blue and white. Inherited cloisonné vase with loose fitting lid, sold for a dollar at the garage sale last autumn to the man with one wandering eye. The orange cat who slept in the wooden bowl. Lawn-side chrysanthemums and that future. Her past spent like matches. The country. One veined and tissued womb. A clam boat caught in a sandbar, the Atlantic Ocean, 1969. The exact corner where his Manhattan apartment was. Mother's hairsprayed wigs taken off the top shelf and the man who set them with the narrow-toothed comb. Assorted terra cotta flower pots, earth-wormed dirt, the garden with nearly every inch growing. One boy's red bicycle. An entire summer. The five years following when I saw her once, worn to wrinkles, in Leasks' underwear department. The actual way it was before the memory of it. How light ribboned entering the room, not wavery but almost solid. Her Too-ra-loo-ra-loo-ral and how I leaned back all the way home on the train. Then all of her, sung patience and distraction, Valentine lipstick, her voice in a sudden story.

Clean Underwear

You go to school because you must learn the rules.
You read books because they are your only true companions.
You walk and do not run.
Do not drink from public water fountains.
We are never *that* thirsty.
You come home because your mother needs you.
You eat leftovers because so many in the world are starving.
Always wear clean underwear.
If they have to pull you out of a wreck, even if you're dead
at least your underwear will be clean.
Carry a dime to call home.
You are trustworthy and never tell the family secrets
or your mother will no longer love you.
You say, "How do you do?"
because you have been raised well,
and answer, "Fine, thank you."
because you are *fine, thank you.*
Curtsy, holding the hem of your dress
as you bend your knees slightly.
Keep your manners inside you like a prayer.
You say your prayers at night
kneeling beside the bed so God will protect you.
When answering the telephone,
say, "One moment, please."
The butter knife is only for butter.
The salad plate is only for salad unless it comes later
in the meal, in which case it is for dessert.
The afternoon is the only time you may nap
and only if you are truly tired.
You are always polite, even to mean people.

You know which poems to recite,
and you know when they are necessary.
Cut your fingernails when they are so long
they threaten you in your sleep.
Cut your hair when everyone has begun
to recognize you.
Shave your legs if the man you sleep with
is the man you love.
Leave your father before he falls.
Leave your man before he leaves you.
You may tell your mother anything.
You must thank her for having raised you well,
so that you may move through the world
knowing you will not make a drastic mistake.
You will not make a mistake as drastic as the one
your mother made by marrying your father
and bearing the children she didn't want
and then drinking herself to death.

No-Child Has A Mother

No-Child's mother is tired again.
If she wore an apron, she would wring it
between her hands. No-Child's mother
has no children to slow her down.

She picks up babies in other mothers' carriages,
holds them the right way and sings old lullabies
to soothe them, to calm herself.

In the dark room she lights candles, and suppers
with No-Child's father. When he drives away
in the morning, she puts on lipstick
hurries to work.

There is No-Child to come home to, no clothes
to wash except her own, no one to cradle or to feed,
no one to scold or to laugh with but herself
and she is too tired.

No-Child Has A Father

No-Child's father picks up his keys
like a small medal and walks toward the door.
He reaches to kiss No-Child's mother
and, as many times before
he opens the door.

The man is a father without children.
He thinks of the woman
and the child they do not have
and he loves them.

Progeny

All the other women at the table had babies, or were
going to any month now. So the men had babies too,
pride glowing through the bowls of their pipes.

With the good food came satisfied laughter, the promise
of a picture window; conversation held their tongues
in its folds. One baby swung far back in the rocker
yet did not fall. He was all blond, and everyone was fair
to him, settling on him, his cheeks pink and his eyes blue.
At the head of the table sat the elder man whose kindly eyes
were frosted. Across from him, his wife touched the silver
and glassware, plates with their green scalloped edges,
what was lost.

Moist, but no longer clotted or sodden, no longer filled
with possibility, I floated above. My lover kept his hand
on my forearm, steadying what was and might have
been, had the weight not been undone and the picture
sewn up, not unlike my body that was put back together.
On the outside, seventeen staples across a thick seam,
pink all the way down.

Sugarmother's Daughter Dreams

These are the same hands that stroke my head in fever.
But no. Her upper lip and teeth protrude over her chin.
An indentation runs from lip to cheekbones
as though she wore a metal bit in her mouth
when she was young, the bones still soft and forming.

She pushes my head back, pulls my hair. I watch the white
ceiling for pigeons to unfold and push her hands away.
But no birds become flesh and wing from plaster.
Holding a pink ten-pound bag, she pours sugar
down my throat so quickly I can't swallow,
my mouth filling like a leather jug,
the sugar overflowing. Her eyes spin out of focus
like a machine above my head. I choke
on the sweetness, the sugar falling on my shoulders
down the front of my blouse.

What horse are you mother, with the bit marks
on your face? What devil, yanking my head back so far?
If I could lift my hand to my forehead
I would make the sign of the cross, ask for forgiveness,
God, so that my real mother would return
in her blue dress and sandals.
But my arms are frozen at my sides, held down by her
grasping, by the sugar, the weight of the sugar
pouring down my black throat.

The Finite and the Infinite

Dressed in black, she spends the evening with him.
Winding her arm through the crook of his, she settles
cautiously against him, and they talk. Will he steal
her pulse? She fears that something of him
may be seeping into her, silent as snow.

Birds call to the darkness, remind her of what is stuck,
crusted in her throat: a silhouette about to speak.

He appears to be a man she could lean into,
says he is unafraid. But she knows fear is hidden
beneath the scar that goes from one side of his belly
all the way to the other, not in what was taken
but in what remains.

She is afraid that his presence will keep her awake
all night. The lights in her room go on
and there is her mother sitting at the desk
typing away on a rusted IBM Selectric.
Her mother would do this to her. Listening
to the keyboard, she gives up on sleep, curls away
from the man's large, soft, sleeping body,
remembers that as a girl when she'd leave for school
her mother would be at the typewriter
and when she came home she'd still be there,
on her tenth or eleventh cup of murky coffee, typing
somebody else's words on onion skin paper—
onehundredeightythree words per minute
and they'd come out looking so appealing.

It takes all night, the mother with her daughter's words,
clattering and pounding them into the machine.
Blowing Chesterfield smoke into the room,

she hands them back, says, "Here, darling, your words."
Under her breath: "Here, your white gloved words,
your silver polished words. Put them on the back of his truck,
see if the wind doesn't take them away.
See where he'll take you. Nowhere, again."

What is the infinite he speaks of that they may
make together?

Will they sit down at the typewriter, napkins on their laps
and eat the words that catch on fire? Will they eat
what is spoken? Will her mother be silent
for once? They are kissing; he is holding her.

Is he sleeping? Does he know that her light is on?

Girlfriend of the Ferry Crossings

for Amber

Lopez Island, the end of August,
and there's nowhere we have to be.
The two of us barefoot on the slanted kitchen floor
of our rented bungalow with the archipelago view.
We are radio sisters, lilting our way
through the one about Billy boy and the cherry pie,
poor boy, who couldn't leave his mother.
Then you are Maria, and I join in, substituting pretty
with another rhyming word, until you cajole me
into the right word, convincing me
at least for the moment, of my own beauty.
Crooning together, we laugh as much as sing,
exaggerating the maudlin parts,
there in our pajamas, hips touching,
a ketchup bottle for a microphone,
inappropriate behavior, perhaps,
for two women approaching middle-age.

Then, quickly dressed and in the car to the spot
where yesterday, on bicycle,
I'd spotted bushes laden with berries.

Staining our hands purple-black, we return
with fruit enough for more than one pie.
The whole-wheat crust I make resembles
toasted sawdust but we eat it anyway,
quenched by juice of berries and vanilla ice cream.

In the evening, I walk the spit dividing the sound
from the lagoon at the edge of the yard
where birds wheel and lift, fill the sky.

All week you've named them upon first glance:
wood thrush or osprey,
you pointed to sky or marsh, noted the color
of the head, which identifies, great blue heron,
sparrow. "Common sparrow," you sighed, regretting
that common should describe any bird.

Over these years we have sheltered
one another many times: at the hospital
when my mother was dying, your last break-up
when I considered slashing his tires,
and most recently your illness,
when, helpless, all I could do was sit with you.

Along this thin ribbon of land I walk
toward the places we have yet to travel,
think of where the days will take us,
lines of songs we don't yet know the tunes to.

Lightning and the Autumn Rain

for Ali

Autumn's first rain has lightning, thunder
knocking through the darkening sky.
Around the dinner table we eat summer
salads, the last toast to the year's rest
from the hurry of days. Quickly
darkness becomes the sky.

Two children sit across from me, following
each flash of lightning, counting the number
of miles the storm is away from our dinner.
Six friends at table; the cook, having flung off
her apron, sits down; the baba ganouj startling
in its abundance of garlic.

A grown-up asks a child, "What are the three things
you cannot live without?"
For her first choice she answers, "Life."
Her next two choices are friendship and garlic.
The three essentials.
Until her young friend says, "Health."
I think, smart again. All the things I take
for granted. My three choices? Immortality.

But my friend's husband, who had forgotten
the question, wants memory as one of his three.
Memory, another thing I have assumed.
Where would I be without that back-turning
glance down the lengthening path?

We are all *in* this dinner, eating our way
through the rain, thunder and lightning;
the floury French bread whitening my lips.
In the background, ballet music plays.

The two girls lift their arms, dance to be
ballerinas when they grow up. Memory.

When I was six I danced on an old wooden
stage, one in a chorus of life-sized flowers.
Afterward my father gave me roses;
I'm sure they were his idea.
Mother pressed the bouquet between pages in a book.
Often I cracked the pages to be sure I had danced that night
the pink bow whitening as the years fled.

Future sits across from me: two eight-year-old girls.
Again lightning flickers through trees, then strikes
wildly above us. And thunder. The girls count.
Four miles away. Later I walk home,
pass college students dancing in the street.

How many choices did she say? Water.
Memory. Health. Only the water can I hold.
And once swallowed, it is invisible as memory,
which is all that exists now of last night's dinner.
My friend, having flung off her apron,
sits down. There she is, the rain coming down,
the evening that was inside us, all our wishes,
and the garlic we ate on the bread.

Our Friday Night

for Michael

Sprawled halfway, we sat together on the couch
before the fire, my living room this time,
late evening, at the end of a particularly long week,
the look of too many things to remember
brimming in your eyes, when the smell of burning
rushed me to the kitchen.
It was the eggplant that was to have been dipped
in sesame seeds, covered with grated parmesan,
and bedded down on the golden spaghetti squash
sauteed with garlic that we would have eaten
with the bulgur, baking also at 350 degrees.

You were so delicate about the burned dinner
that I had wanted to give you, kissing
my face everywhere, my eyes and ears
and hair even, kissing over
my apologizes for the dinner now uneatable.
It could have been so much worse than my plans
to please you gone to ashes, more than eggplant,
thinly sliced, going up in smoke.

This morning, the baking sheet washed clean,
your kisses decorate my face still.
True, bread and salad served us well.
May I please you often, and your kisses,
may they linger.

Restaurant

That fast kiss moves
from her neck to mine.

She leaves her name off the letter
and pretends to be hidden in the lake.

Splashing water on her face,
the water is not warm enough.

It would be better to start
on this side if you want to find her,

where the climb is more gradual.
That's what he's fighting with.

Their legs underneath the table
almost touch.

Spelling Lesson at Thirty-Seven

Often I forget how to spell certain words,
despite my delight in their meanings.
Take dessert and desert; I know that one
is sweet, follows dinner
and the other
is a wide expanse of sand,
long hot days, little water
yet I confuse the arrangement of their letters.
So on my shopping list, quickly written,
I have *desert.*
And what I come home with is not the sun
burning down on a desolate place,
but a white box holding layers of glazed
slivered almonds, set in a flaky crust.
Spelled either way,
my friends, who arrive late
but have not deserted me, sit down and
eat with their fingers
while I am distracted by the heat,
thinking about a certain man,
wondering how to spell
what we are.
Is this what I deserve,
reward or punishment,
my *just desserts?*
One day he arrived before dinner
at the pre-arranged hour
and yet was, himself, dessert—milk and honey.
And this week,
without even the briefest consonance
of his voice, has been desert-like.
I behave like the wind,
knock over obstacles in my path.

There is barely enough water
for drinking.
My friends, knowing nothing
about the sweetness and heat
he has put into my body, eat on.
Hungry, a woman travels the desert
across miles of sand,
unsure of
her direction,
which letters will take her where.

Sotto, Sotto

In the movie when the two Italian women
wearing tight dresses and black heels
look at each other their lips quiver
and I get lonely.
It enters through the thickness
of my covered thighs, flows like a river.
I don't know if I'm aching for the dark
haired woman, the light haired
woman, the moustached husband
or all the ancient stone buildings of Rome.

At the funny parts, everyone
in the theatre laughs, though none
as loudly and coarsely as I.
Laughter rises from my belly,
slips through my throat and
pours into the velvet room, falling
over the chairs.

I don't want to hold your hand.
I want to be lonely and to laugh
and for the laughter to break
inside me like birds taking flight
under the Italian sky.

Everything, and I Don't Know How

A blond hair floats
in the coffee cup.
Lift it out and it disappears,
no proof.

"You make it difficult," she says
and I remember nothing.

It's the way I write my name,
wear my hair.

It's the way I want
that makes me troublesome,
moving my whole self into it.

Unforgivable,
here's a handful of sins
I can count on.

What Grandmother Wants

She wants me to sign my name to our life.
And I won't. She wants you to slip
the ring onto my finger, to see the gold
shimmer, to know I will be taken care of.
You should give me the key
to a new car, a house. I won't do it.

She wants her dinner and her baby-rattle
teeth so she can eat. I have to sing
to hide the horrible sound. And I won't.
But baby, put your head here
on my smooth chest,
on my flat, whispering heart,
and I will stroke your black hair,
and then we can make the bed
while grandmother hangs on to
my voice that she can not hear.

I hold to her life which is three thousand
miles away and as small as the girl
who married her future to the man
from the old country
who'd courted her for two weeks.

And later she said, "Finally, I did love him."
But she didn't say when, for how long or why.

II

What lasts is what you start with.
—Charles Wright

The Sadness I Live For

for Rose Vecchione

Grandmother's teeth sleep without her
in the blue box beside the bathroom sink
and greet me at night in their shiny silence
when I stumble across the aging floorboards
of grandmother's house.

Those porcelain teeth will outlast you, Grandma,
and without you they cannot speak
of traveling across Manhattan by horse,
of the boy born on the kitchen table,
or the tiny baby lost to influenza.
I can not fit those teeth into my own mouth
when you are gone, gone.

Early summer mornings, you wheel out
to the living room, your ancient half-legs
covered. Ghost of a woman,
you are my only hero. It's breakfast
and another television day beside the rumbling
air conditioner. I fall asleep in your presence,
dream of you, only twenty-five years ago,
the fine grandma you were, your homemade
spaghetti drying on the bed.

This year you will give me, maybe,
one more story, and I will ask for it, over
and over, again. I'll tell you stories of the family
I met last summer in the old country, the woman
who has grandpa's very own face, my skin, yours.

You'll hand me another string of pearls
left over from the thin years of tripe for dinner
or a bean soup, when you strung beads for money.
The fake strand will be longer this year,
as I am older, more deserving of your gems,
and the gold-threaded dresses I am too thin to wear.

Grandma, you are our history alive.
And when you are gone, you'll be more
than my hero; you'll be the end of a world,
the sadness I live for.

Astoria, New York, 1988

Late into the night my father rummages
in the basement of the house beside the East River,
heaving Christmas paper, crushed metal toys,
and the torn past into black plastic bags.

This is no longer his home; he is the visiting son.
Through dusty, turn of the century books, old Italian letters,
furs and sequined dresses, the tools his father made
from iron and wood, he digs.

My father wraps and buries this hot summer
night deep among rags. When he raises his voice,
something broken falls down the stairs: the dead father,
the dead sister, the mother who wants him and cries,
the mother he makes cry.

Climbing through the decades of dirt, from the beginning
of this house, from the lost teeth of his boyhood,
in the hollow room, he shrinks
and grows tall again, becomes not my father,
shouts at the garbage, calls it names.

Upstairs his mother rolls back and forth
in her wheel chair. This does not hurt him.
And it does.

My Father's Hands

Sitting at water's edge, I stroke my father's hands,
their cool limpness, to weight his tapered fingers
down where the moons rise perfectly.
The cancer's been drugged back, but the body
holds disease still within its slackness.

His skin is milky, eyes pale. His gaze wanders back
to an earlier time, New York in the 30's, the color
of light against the buildings.

Past anything else to say, we look toward the cliffs
or at nothing, but not each other.

Over and over I reach for my father's hands,
for what was once there, what we wait for,
what may not return.

First Communion

I.

I have been in this photograph for seventeen years,
dressed like a miniature bride, holding a bouquet
with both hands, white and yellow flowers,
as if I'd been trained to hold them this way.
"Look at yourself in the mirror now,"
my mother says, "You will never see yourself
in a veil again." I am eight years old.

Hands pull at the folds of my white dress.
What the photograph does not show,
what the photographer refuses to see:
My father has gone to a new city.
He mistakes those hands pulling at his tie for love.
She says he has made too many mistakes.

I lose my voice in what I say. Borrow the girl
for the photograph. Tell her you love her
this way, she is certainly pretty enough.
The kitchen table was so clean after dinner.
We sat down with everything spread open.
And oh, the little girl was clean too.

At night they leave the lights on. I draw pictures
in the air and make tunnels, crawl down
into the blankets where I get lost burying myself,
until the angry man hears me crying
and he comes in, smiling.

A hundred little girls walk down the aisle
of the church, complacent, quiet as dolls.
We had practiced the walk, invented sins
to tell the wooden priest. I could never tell
the hidden man what I'd really done.

There isn't actually a first memory;
rather there exists a collection of things
all happening at the same time. I can't distinguish
anyone in the picture, except for myself and a series
of formless shadows whispering through the trees.

II.
In first grade our teachers are the nuns
who cover themselves in black gowns, their words
are polite and compressed.
Even at seven, I do not like looking like
everyone else: a school of children dressed
like military men.
My braids are especially long, thick
and tightly woven.

School wouldn't be so bad,
except for all the other kids who don't want
to play with me and with whom I don't really want to play.

"This is the way to hold your hands,
like a sign towards God."
I mouth the prayers, refusing to memorize
what I do not understand.
After a while of watching the really fat girl sway back
and forth as she prays, I learn the words.
It is easier this way.

Cutting the skin at the back of my mouth,
I make my gums bleed, anything
to be let out for a little while, a drink of water
to stop the blood. If only for some untampered air,
something to remind me.

After school I like to walk down the hill ahead
of all the other girls. Their voices follow me
like a choir, like a veil. My thighs rub together
and stick. I do not think of myself as fat.

III.
The family will move to Chicago. What is Chicago?
I like surprises. An airplane is like a boat that flies.
There will be new streets, a dark brick walk-up,
unfamiliar rooms.

Before leaving our apartment, I take a lipstick
from Mommy's purse, walk into my empty bedroom
closet, echoes falling over me. Up and down on the walls,
as high as I can reach, I write words
I've learned in school: away, going, goodbye,
and the secret words I've made up. Wide, looping
letters, long scribbled red words,
until they are ready, call my name.
Then I shut the door, leave
the girl behind.

Family Standing Nowhere

The late summer fields,
dirtied yellow along the highway,
stretch beyond fence posts
and telephone poles toward a far away
the family will never see
at the edge of the photograph
where the clouds slip low.

This is the middle of Nebraska:
no houses or schools, no arguments
or parents who never kiss.
They have stopped here
for a picture.

In his black raincoat, the father stands:
black framed glasses, hands in pockets,
shoulders hunching forward.

The stalwart mother, hair held
from the wind in a net kerchief,
invokes a smile as if this were a picture
taken in absolving light.

She reaches through the loop
in her husband's arm and with the other arm
presses her younger daughter close,
the girl nuzzling against her
mother's hollowness,
their lengthening shadows tilting
back on the asphalt.

To include as much nowhere
as the frame will hold, the older daughter
stands at a distance with the camera,

angry at her parents for leaving home
behind them, Chicago, where she played
horses on the midway.

She waits to click the button
until they are cold and tired of standing
ready to be passing through the plains;
the birds, prairie dogs and grasses
they will not notice
as they travel in the small car
that holds their singing; songs
promising that the good past
will surround them in the next state.
Once there, the older daughter will join
the photograph, and the long shadows
will slip back into their bodies.
The father will take off his coat,
the little sister will run and jump,
and stories will claim
the mother's voice again.

Kitchen Table Waltz

In the dark background, I'm the one girl orchestra
sitting in the chair against the wall playing music
for them to dance.

They are my parents, floating their yardstick bodies
across the floor. I think of love, how this must be
what I dream of. My sister isn't born yet,
though she too is in the audience
watching from the forest.

My father holds my mother in his arms.
His hands coo up and down her skinny back.
Bending her head, she laughs into his shoulder.

Later, as she tucks my covers in, she will ask,
"And what have you done today?"
I've grown hungry sitting at the table
set aglow with plastic food.

At the end of the dance, as the music cools
I clap from the outside, my sister from the inside.
We applaud the dancers who have worn
their groove in the yellow linoleum floor.

In my party hat and black patent leather shoes
I stand on the table clapping, until at last
they face me and shyly take their perfect bow.

Henny Besmartney

You were the jewel of my childhood, the glitter
my mother scorned, sign of a cheap woman.
Your bracelets sliding up and down your chubby arms
charmed me, jingling together like coins
in your husband Max's pockets.
A ten dollar bill was folded into a dice-sized square
enclosed in plastic, in case you were ever stranded.
Beside the Star of David it swayed on the silver chain.
The pinks and oranges of your full-skirt dresses
shimmered brilliant as stars.
When Max played Bach's *Chaconne* on violin for me,
my baby cries would hush, his nicotined fingers
made the violin sing.

Once your dress shop got tangled in flames
of polyester; a fire burst into the satin
and crinoline, the silver buttons and zippers.

And now, years later, when I call your number,
Ravenswood 9-6017, a bank teller answers.
You've gone to ashes too, to smoke sheer as gauze.
You're a glimmer at the edge of me
so hushed away, like the subway rides
we took, and the huge noise
of the trains trying to eat our voices
and swallow them for good.

Anger's Gift

Grandmother, who kept her own teeth
all eighty-nine years of her life,
kept her anger longer. She has it,
even now, in the company of angels
and lambs. Grandmother used her anger
like spit to make the family move,
the screen door shaking on its hinge.
She used it to bend my mother's back,
to make her hair fall out, every last stitch.
Without losing any, she gave it away
to her daughters, the way some women
pass on tatted doilies or remedies
to soothe stiff feet.
And my mother used her inheritance
well and long, when she called me
fat pig in front of my school-girl friend,
and when she chased my sister around
the house with a knife in one hand.
Early on she passed it to me, the fire stick
I will juggle all my life.
During the day I wear it in my dress pocket,
try to keep it down, tamed a little.
At night, sometimes, it comes out
and I don't sleep.
I watch it get big in the room and
surround me, so that I beg God
and the angels to save me
from the family heirloom.
They sing the Gloria and Ave Maria
to shrink the anger until it is only
one brick-hard loaf of bread
that I don't know who would eat.

My Mother Is A Horse

Mother, your voice is freezing. It is winter enough
for a fire. I want to see you every day.

Someday they will call to say she is dead.
My eyes are on backwards. My history is upside down.
"Who is your mother?" they will ask.

My mother is a horse; just look at her hands,
knuckles swelling like small balloons. Her fingers
ache. She cannot bend them. I fold them for her.
But I will no longer pour her drinks
from the nightly bottles of wine. Mother.

You are gone again. And I can not watch you
dying slowly this way. Soon you won't be able
to focus your eyes, your feet will grow too stiff
to carry you as far as the bed. Oh, Mother.

You wanted to be a saint. And you are a drunk instead.

Salt

Salt has collected along my eyelids
from some sleep I must have cried in
some sadness I love only at night.
In Gram's Boston rocker, the arms worn
through the black paint to the natural wood
I sit, rocking back and forth.
Along my eyelids salt rubs off in flakes
layer after layer of dried tears.
And the sorrow that wore the rocker
through how many coats of paint
where did that come from
to whom did it first belong
and why is it now mine?

Our Private Air

We think back through our mothers, if we are women.
                                                    —*Virginia Woolf*

I'm living in town again
and we don't see much of each other.
Yet few days go by when I don't think of you.
Memory returns to my fingers when I reach
to smooth my hair. Sometimes we talk
for an hour, and we have everything to say.
Another orchid has bloomed in your yard,
and you want to scream again
about the way things are at the office.

If I could give you anything more,
would there ever be enough for us?
Yesterday when we drove to Carmel, I worried
about the silence which might sit between us
in the warm November air if either of us ran out
of things to say, but our voices never stopped.
At the corner our bodies turned together.
Before crossing we held hands.
Looking into shop windows
we liked the same things, nearly every time.

When I was four we walked through snowy
streets in uptown Manhattan, Saturday afternoons
around Christmas. We never lost each other then.
You were the most beautiful woman alive,
and walking with you was heaven.
I was your only one, *the prettiest girl
in the world,* you sang.
I thought if you died, I'd go with you.

Driving home through Monterey
up to your house, I want to stay longer,
but have someplace else to go.
When you open the door, we become
strangers. I forget how to kiss you
and just keep waving until I turn
the corner onto on another street.

Hospital Mask Poem

This is a mask you're wearing:
wires, bruises, oxygen,
all pain in your bald face.
Your grey eyes hide from me
beneath this tomb of illness.

Somebody's singing soprano
in a happier room down the hall.
I'm singing lullabies and baseball songs
to bring you back.

Straining to birth you,
I bear down, breathe.
Empty, I am unable to lure the sickness
from the white sack of your body.

A Month Later

A month later, and still I find hospital kleenex
in my pockets, the jacket I pulled on the night
you gave your body away.

This morning there are clouds
and a hesitant breeze,
and you are not anywhere my mother,
except everywhere: in the shifting of my spirit,
in my legs tightly crossed.

Your steel eyes melted during those last days
as you became only the good mother.

I hang a picture of you in my house.
The girl you were before I was born
dies every time I look
at her soft face.

When Grief Moves In

It happens in the car, or
standing in place, those moments in between things,
when the eyes shift, before finding focus again.
There, at the edge of conversation.

And such room grief has taken, caused me
to move twice in an attempt to house her.
My body is not big enough.

The sadness of my bones cracks and snaps
in the hold of her hunger.

Four Months

My life falls in a pile on the bedroom floor.
Some days it's all I can do to pull the sheets
and blankets up.
I sign my name over and over,
write letters to old family friends,
explain my mother's death.
I say brain hemorrhage. I say stroke.
I say better dead than half living.
How do I know this? I don't.

Her blue sweater. Her strand of pearls.
Her scent in my rooms, alive.

I Come to You Empty-Handed

I come to you empty-handed,
no flowers for your grave,
nothing to bridge
the gates of our worlds, only
the small pit of my heart
knocking fiercely
against flesh and bone.

Nine Months

The world is a tunnel
without you:
hollow,
no mother,
no one to do good for
but myself
and she is so tiny.

Her Face in the Trees

The grey fog holds her face, and trees move into it
there at the far side of the park, across the slow
street, beyond children out playing in the rain.
Up above, tree limbs are bent and buoyed,
leaves float on the wind.

It's a late Saturday afternoon as I sit thinking of her,
unable to remember her last words to me, spoken
eight years ago. Perhaps they were the words
of the Irish lullaby, which were also the first she gave me
when I was only a tiny thing, and for hours
she would rock me till sleep came.

At the end I rocked her, straddling the bed,
her head in my hands, then arms fully around her.
It was April. We were both younger then.
It does not surprise me that our last words
would have been a song.

How much of her I don't remember. And how she rises now,
an apparition, above the trees in the town of her dying
where she was never really at home, not city enough
for her here, and where years before
she let her eldest daughter go, told me to never
call her mother again.

But that is another song, the one framing this story,
that is forever behind me, nipping,
never clean. I lie back against the pillows
the hearth's fire rushing through the wood
this late April storm, tree limbs arch and tip,
bend into the clouded wind.

Mother, you are the lost shadow
I carry everywhere, the voice at the edge

of me, flickering at times, firelike.
Return to me the lullaby we held between us,
words to a song those wind blown trees have, your face,
a mirage I look for and see wavering in them.

III

A memory of love disguised as a meadow...
—Vladimir Nabokov

Tree

An afternoon
that is almost evening
the sky almost an ocean.
And us, intimate as trees
rooted in the same earth
until a fire unravels the dust.
I am a moment in one tree
not a small bird
not a leaf that makes
the wind sing.

Acacia

When the acacia are in blossom
we wake together in your room.
Sun-yellow buds ignite February's
false spring with their light
while a stray dog wanders
lost in the desert of my heart.
Through the four red rooms
she searches for a river
that rushes and is still.

Are you this body of water
or a tree on the bank
in bloom?

For the Wave

My arms are the breath
of the body that feeds you.
Hungry swimmers float
in black and white, covering
the soles of your skin.
And the kitchen table tilts
forward and back.

If the plane doesn't land,
if the ground sinks
or doesn't find us whispering
over the crackles of the telephone
and if the whole world ends
I will wait for you.

Until you arrive
my arms will be thirsty
motionless swimmers
waiting for the wave.

Near Spring

Late at night, in a rain-soaked orchard
of sweet almond, in the central valley town
of the baths, you unload the white boxes of bees
from the wide back of your flatbed truck,
set them down in rows beside the twisting trees,
so in the morning the bees will begin turning
the white and pink blossoms into fruit.
Handing me the smoker, you show me how
to heat the bees into making honey in their hives.
Momentarily unafraid, I lean up to the boxes
where nectar rises, floats into the misty air.

Tell me, is this a heat to run from, or do I turn
toward the honeying, the sudden beating
of wings, the hum and buzz of the inner hive?

August's Full Moon

for Michael

Having slipped into summer,
this haphazard, tiddly-winked
fragment of time, mostly
what I do is love you.

In the garden, my hands
pulling at the stubborn weeds
love you. While taking care
of business, long distance
over the telephone,
I am doing it there.
And at the corner market
where the bins are burdened
with corn and strawberries
and the basil that we turn
into suppertime, there too.

That afternoon together
at Pomponio Beach
I loved you, but said only
the word *summer*. Then said it
over again, so you would know
the heat that I was singing about.

Under the Comet's Sky

Circling my waist
you turn me toward you

Between now and morning
the whole quiet is ours

and sleep comes later

In A Corner of the Room

The sky is silver white, and pink
rises from the sea. Bitten by autumn's
newness, the air is. In a corner of the room
sits a house, green shuttered, red roofed,
that my Grandmother made for me
to reach my girl-hands into, setting
the table for tea, rocking the infants
in the rose-starred cradles that she crafted
with her careful fingers, such tiny places
for sleeping. Inside the rooms there is less
light than almost anywhere. The one
who was here last evening pressed
his head against my shoulder,
weeping, and with my hands
I comforted him there.

At the Mountain

Hold my breath
with your blue eyes.
Stroke my fingers
along the shore
of your throat.

I will drink there,
and take your body
past the dip in the road,
where swallows dissolve
into song, then beyond
the roots of trees.

We are not killing
each other,
we are cooling
our mighty thirst.

Night Moths Whispering

Sleeping alongside a creek bed,
my dreams are of water.
When the night winds shudder
down the narrow valley,
my home is taken downstream
past me—doors, window glass, his picture
framed in blue. Is there some place
where I belong?

Patience

Not a fish or a turtle, the river rat swims.
The brown stone of her body glides
from riverside to riverside.
In her mouth she carries water-grass,
the dry stems that border these banks.
She is building a nest, for this is spring's
first day, when babies prepare to be born.

On the wood and silver bridge I stand
looking down and across at the green hills,
the pastureland and at my own solitude
that flickers and chimes like a bell within.

For hours the rat continues, swims
across the river, and again, more grass
in her small mouth.
Just beneath the water's surface
her long tail swirls and the wet fur glistens,
the wake of her effort nearly disappears
each time she reaches the far shore.

At the Gateway to Desolation Wilderness

It is afternoon now, the sun having assumed
its place at the height of the sky, a baked stillness
about this July day. Little movement
except for small flickering waves upon the lake
and the nearly imperceptible glide of wind
through tree branches. Little sound
other than one bird's repeated few syllable call.

For nearly a year, within all the rush and business
of my days, the ones that incessantly hollered,
Hurry, I have waited for a day like this, when everything
appears to linger, the world turning in slow motion
as though nothing bad would ever happen again,
and everything would wait, without impatience,
for everything else, as though this were all there was,
this one any day, this time.

At all the blue and green and brown the summer
afternoon has to offer I look out: swath of lake water
set canyon-deep between two mountain
sides, the stately Lodgepole pines,
the one peak rising to tree-line, its stone
a jutting edge against the bright sky.

Between now and nightfall a bulk of hours
spreads out before me, those recently behind
cluster like shiny beads. It is so still
my mother could be alive.
In the rocker I sit, barely pulsing it back and forth
and a tiny breeze, small as a sleeping child's
breath, comes in through the Dutch door.

There is nowhere I have to go, nearly nowhere
I have ever been, other than here, beside the lake.

Far off a woman's rippling laughter,
once, twice, and then not even the wind's sound.

Hot Springs at Colusa

On days which at quick glance
seemed unremarkable and on days
when it rained so hard traveling down
the dirt road would have been impossible
and at times when it was too warm
to enter even the coolest tub, I have rested
here, but never before in such weather.
The wind's become a gale in no time—
a chilly torrent pushes through the canyon.
In the hottest bath I sit alone,
facing it. Bamboo flails, gold grasses flatten,
pines twist and bend. And darkness comes.
The wind has blown all the clouds away
but not the night's first star, nor the moon
nearly full in the summer sky.

Bear Valley in September

for Gina

All day yesterday I looked for the right words
to describe the color of the fields and hills
surrounding the springs at Sulphur Creek.
There wasn't one that came near what I was seeing.
Ochre, yellow, sand—I tried them aloud
but none would do. The blanched thigh-high grasses:
oat straw and milk thistle, that clutch together
in the wind, lean down at times close to their ground,
brittle and stickery this time of year.
In the day's range of light their color changes.
But never is it butter, nor golden, and not honey,
though with hints of these.

Still wanting to say it, I walked out again at dusk.
The quick gusts of air blew my hair back from my face
the whole way there, and I welcomed that attention.
Dragonflies nearly as large as swallows, flew
over the fields; their sheer, veined wings carrying them.
Rounding bend after bend, I arrived finally at the one place
where the valley opens, and stood before nightfall,
taking the wind into my body and the color of the fields,
which had become something else again, and which,
still, I had no name for.

Toward the Only Sky

In memory of Rosmarie

West of east and south of north, where wind crosses
the miles of fences, loud all the way to the other side
an angel stands, same stance as always, one hip raised,
one foot slightly forward, snake beneath the feet.
The halo above her head is the full moon
glowing incandescent like her tiny carmine lips
visible as she turns her head slightly,
her plaited wings woven from thin tree branches.

The map that leads here she carries under her dress,
the highways which move the blue blood
and the red blood. She knows the world is round:
where her heart used to be there is water
surrounded by a wall of stone, moss covered,
the bluest water.

Cherry Valley, Sun City, where the Mojave
River forks, south of Hesperia, north of Green Valley,
the small roads, tributaries that finger, intersect.
You have to follow the voice here, the only way
is to listen. But one doesn't always.

The ticket to Heaven, it's hers, the woman
in the bed, facing the window,
across from the new church steeple, shiny and black.
She kept hold of my eyes with hers for minutes
at a time. I didn't know how to reassure her
I just kept looking back.
How long does dying take, from the inside, how long?
"What does the ticket look like? How do I use it?"
she asks, looking out toward all the night.
It's out there, the angels who can take you.

She describes a particular blue to me,
like the Swiss Alps, she says, *not on top,*
underneath them, glacier blue. How do you die?
You go underneath the glacial blue and above it.
Make flight yours for once and always. Asking,
is there another side?

In this canyon the wind comes up like a woman
not resigned to her dying. Saying no, it isn't time.
But then it is. Illness in the body says so, how the bad
cells destroy what is good. Squeezing fistfuls
of sheet and blanket, her breathing labors, pauses
too long, labors again. Her lips dry and blistering.

How do you die, let go of what is known, the familiar?
How do you open the shutters and allow the wind inside,
the whole cold wind, let it in? Doorway, path,
black church steeple outside the window
and the bells chime on Sunday.
She will walk the tributaries, fingerings of water
past where the river divides, up the frosted
northern slope, glacial blue,
the underside.

Nearing the Winter Solstice

Along the ridge top, after a hard climb, I walked
to where the rainstorm began, stood for awhile
with one foot on either side, straddling
the boundary of weather, proving, that in fact
you can be in two places at the same time.

In what light remained, I watched nearby
and toward the mountains so faraway
they became black wings, how the light held
what it touched in radiance, so that everything
became all that it could be, all that it was
on the best of days. The trunk of the craggy
manzanita became more certainly red than I had
ever seen before. It seemed to call out, like a bell
to whomever was listening, saying I am this
manzanita tree. And the green blades of grass,
each one, tilting down then rising up, seemed to say
I am this grass, shiny and bright. The enormous wind
that pushed into my ears, made everything move.
Light, like in the paintings of Baby Jesus,
how his face holds it so completely he gives it away
enlivening everything that passes.

Quickly, now that the rain had become hail,
the thick clouds gathering, I walked back down
the ridge, past the cows grazing homeward
past the cold spring rushing, past the fallen barn
musty and hollow, past the dampening fields
spread out in all directions, past everything familiar
which until this light, I had never seen before.

About the Author

Patrice Vecchione's poetry appears in journals and anthologies. She is the editor of *Fault Lines: Children's Earthquake Poetry*. Patrice co-edited *Catholic Girls, Bless Me, Father: Stories of Catholic Childhood,* and *Storming Heaven's Gate: Spiritual Writings by Women* all published by Penguin books. She is the poetry editor for the newspaper, *La Gazette: A Feminist Forum for the Central Coast.*

Through her program, *The Heart of the Word: Poetry and the Imagination,* Patrice has taught poetry along California's central coast for over twenty years. She consults and lectures nationally. Patrice has lead workshops for local community groups such as The Central California Writing Project, The Homeless Garden Project in Santa Cruz, and The Pajaro Valley Shelter Services, as well as for the Monterey and Santa Cruz county libraries. She has been a radio host for Santa Cruz's KUSP: the National Public Radio Affiliate for the Central Coast, broadcasting a children's program called *Castle Cottage* and a poetry show.

Patrice co-produces the benefit *In Celebration of the Muse,* an annual poetry and prose reading by Santa Cruz women writers. In 1997, she co-edited an anthology for the event's fifteenth anniversary, published as an issue of University of California at Santa Cruz's *Quarry West.*

A past resident of Santa Cruz, Patrice currently lives in Monterey, California, and regularly travels between the two counties along the bay.

colophon

Designed and printed by Kate Hitt, using offset and letterpress methods at Many Names Press, 3110-B Porter Street, Soquel, California 95073. Four-color scan and film output for the cover by Prism Photographics in Santa Cruz. Annie Browning set the type in Minion roman, italic, and semibold 10/14 with Cochin, and contemporary digital faces Ultra Condensed Serif and OPTICarmella Handscript used for various accents.

This limited edition of 800 was printed on Fraser Synergy 80# laid text, recycled and acid-free, using soy-based inks.